D0460924

Molly's New
Washing Machine

For my mother—who listened when
all I could say was, "Ab ab ab."

Molly's New Washing Machine
Text copyright © 1986 by Laura Geringer
Illustrations copyright © 1986 by Petra Mathers
Printed in the U.S.A. All rights reserved.

Library of Congress Cataloging-in-Publication Data
Geringer, Laura.
  Molly's new washing machine.

  Summary: Molly and her friends, running a test load
of laundry in her mysterious new washing machine,
dance to the music it makes during its cycles.
  [1. Laundry—Fiction.   2. Dancing—Fiction]
I. Mathers, Petra, ill.   II. Title.
PZ7.G296Mo 1986   [E]   85-45839
ISBN 0-06-022150-X
ISBN 0-06-022151-8 (lib. bdg.)

Designed by Constance Fogler
1 2 3 4 5 6 7 8 9 10
First Edition

Molly's New Washing Machine

by **LAURA GERINGER** · illustrated by **PETRA MATHERS**

HARPER & ROW, PUBLISHERS

One day Molly looked out her kitchen window.

Two rabbits stood there. They looked very strong. Molly opened the door.

"Here's your new washing machine," said one.

"Where should we put it?" asked the other.

"Anywhere," Molly said, surprised.

The machine had a round window like the porthole of a ship. It was white and shiny. Molly hadn't ordered it, but she liked its looks immediately.

"I guess I better plug it in," she thought when the rabbits had gone.

6.

But nothing happened.

Just then, Bongo walked in. "It needs soap," he said.

"Of course it does," said Molly, and she dug under the sink.

"Bottoms up," said Bongo, and they poured.

Molly flipped the switch. A red light went on and off, on and off.

"Is it just going to *blink* at me?" asked Molly.

"Kick it," growled Bongo.

He was about to do just that when there was a knock on the door.

8.

There was Click, his chest puffed out like Superman. Slowly, he circled the washing machine.

"It needs clothes," he said.

Molly slipped off her apron and tossed it into the machine.

"Now you," she told Bongo.

Bongo blushed but gave her his sweatshirt and his wig.

"You too, Click," said Molly.

Click bowed from the waist.

"Step and stride and straddle ho,

   Rigadoon and do-si-do," he said.

"None of that nonsense," said Molly. "Let's have your socks. And your gloves, too."

"Socks it is—the lady wants socks," said Click, and he untied his shoes and fed his socks to the machine. Then he peeled off his gloves.

"All set," said Molly.

10.

But there was Pocket at the door.

"You're just in time, Pocket," yelled Molly.

"Wobble bobble, don't be late,

   Fickle faddle, you're the bait," said Click.

"The bait for what?" asked Pocket warily.

"Don't listen to him," said Molly. "Just watch the washing machine."

"If it works," said Bongo.

"Will it clean my bow tie?" asked Pocket.

"Sure," said Molly. "Give it here."

So Pocket added his bow tie to the bundle. Then he took off his glasses, polished them on his shirt, and placed them carefully back on his nose. He bent closer to the washing machine.

"Look at all these buttons," he breathed. "They're different colors."

"Let's press the yellow one," said Bongo. "It says SOAK."

12.

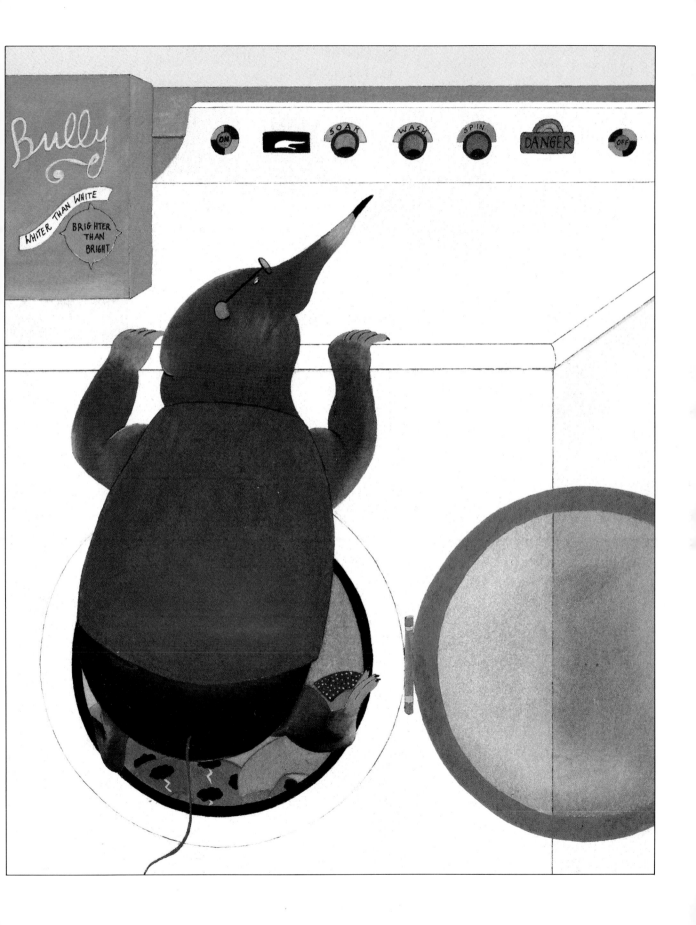

Ab ab ab, said the machine.

"Listen!" Molly whispered.

Nima pui pui pui.

"Oh, listen to that," Molly cried, and she skipped across the room.

Toot toot totto toot.

Molly picked up the corner of her skirt and shook it at Bongo.

"Let's dance!" she yelled.

Nud nud nud, zegga zegga.

Click snapped his fingers, Pocket clapped, and they all swirled around Molly's kitchen.

"Ping and pong and hide and seek,

  Swing your partner cheek to cheek," sang Click, waving his arms. Then he strutted up to Molly and led her in a cha cha cha.

Molly's hair flopped in all directions as they did the cha cha all around Molly's kitchen.

No one noticed Penelope at the window.

14.

Pepi pu pepi pu, pu pu pepi pu.

"It's changing," warned Molly as a little green light began to gleam.

"We're in wash time now," barked Bongo.

He spun Molly away from Click and all around the room.

"Can't beat the beat!" said Click.

"Nothing like it," Pocket agreed.

And they both joined in, doing a jig.

Poot zurn poot zurn, poot poot zurn zurn zurn.

They pooted and zurned all around Molly's kitchen.

"Let's jump!" Molly shouted. So they jumped up on top of one another's shoulders and jumped all around Molly's kitchen.

And Penelope watched through the window.

16.

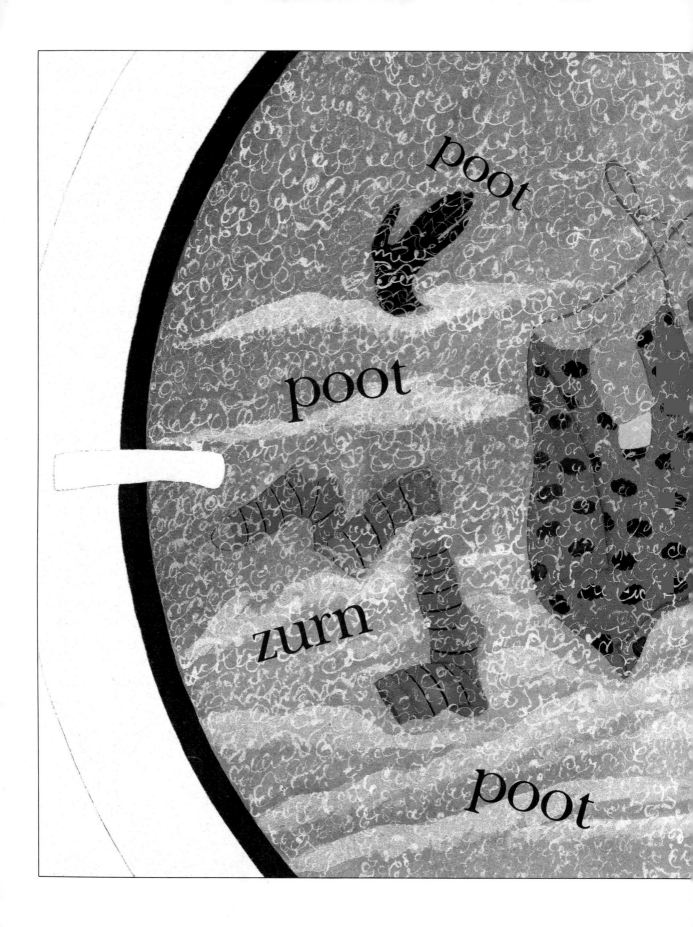

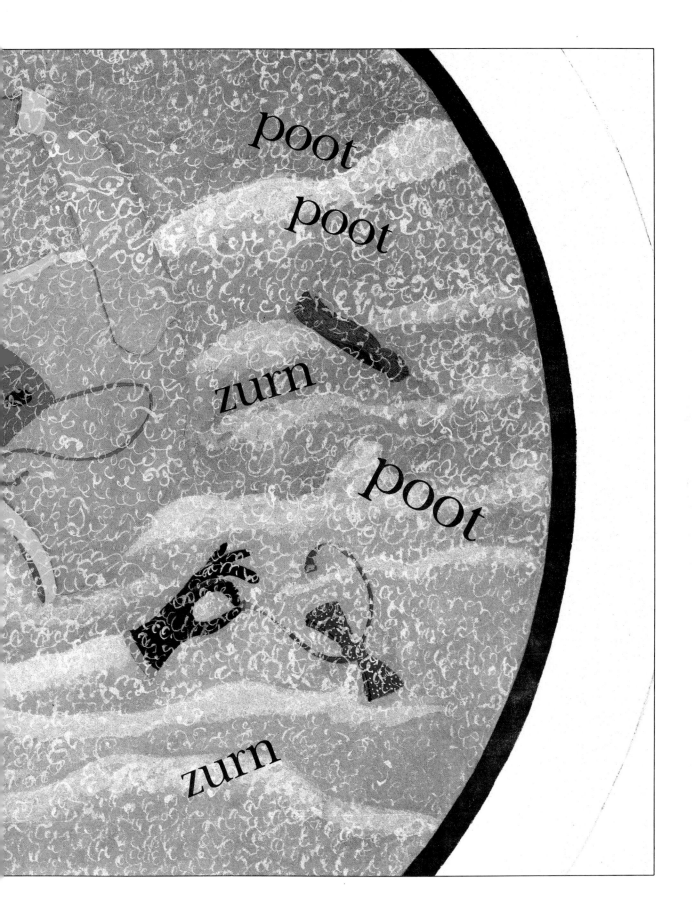

"Stop!" panted Bongo. "I'm out of breath."

"Can't!" gasped Molly.

"No stopping now," puffed Pocket.

"Double shuffle, paw the ground,

Keep it going, move around.

Pinch your gal and double back,

Murka zurka, quack quack quack," chanted Click.

He wasn't out of breath at all.

But the washing machine was playing a different
tune again.

Ug ug nuk nuk, nuk ug nuk ug nuk, it went, and all its
lights—the red, the yellow, and the green—began to pop
and flash at once.

Uh…Uuh…Uuuuh, choked the machine as soap
spurted out the front.

"Suds!" shrieked Molly.

"Bubbles!" yelped Bongo.

"Froth!" squealed Pocket.

"Yesssss," hissed Click contentedly.

And they slipped and slid all around Molly's sudsy
kitchen.

And Penelope watched, too shy to come inside.

20.

"Frolic rolic I declare,

   Push your partner, pull her hair," chimed Click,

switching into two-step.

   "But it's rinse time!" Molly laughed, tippy-tapping

after him.

   They swayed and sashayed all around Molly's kitchen

until Molly threw back her head, shut her eyes, and leaped

clear across the room.

   "Drops are flying, 'cause we're spin drying," she

whooped. Then she turned and turned and turned in a

big, broad circle until she could no longer say for sure if

she was in her own kitchen or not.

   Bongo started circling too, and so did Click and Pocket,

all turning round and round until they couldn't say for

sure what was up and what was down.

   Penelope wished she could spin too.

   22.

Zut, said the machine. And it stopped.

"Ung!" said Molly.

"Oof!" said Bongo.

"Ump!" said Click, not rhyming for once.

"Eh?" asked Pocket.

And they all tumbled in a heap on the floor of Molly's kitchen.

Penelope ran away.

"That was good," said Molly.

"I'm all done in," said Bongo.

"I'm hot," said Click.

"Let's cool off," said Pocket.

And he went to open the door.

There stood the same two rabbits.

"Sorry," said one. "We had the wrong place."

"Excuse us," said the other, politely.

And they lifted Molly's new washing machine onto their big, broad shoulders and grunted out of Molly's kitchen...

28.

all the way down the block to…

Penelope's house!